ARTHUR SLADE

Villainology

Fabulous Lives of

the Big, the Bad,

and the Wicked

Illustrated by Derek Mah

Tundra Books

*For the Wicked Witch of the East, who taught
the world the importance of fashionable shoes.* – A.S.

For every villain who knows they didn't do it. – D.M.

Text copyright © 2007 by Arthur Slade
Illustrations copyright © 2007 by Derek Mah

Published in Canada by Tundra Books,
75 Sherbourne Street, Toronto, Ontario M5A 2P9

Published in the United States by Tundra Books of Northern New York,
P.O. Box 1030, Plattsburgh, New York 12901

Library of Congress Control Number: 2006909137

Library and Archives Canada Cataloguing in Publication

Slade, Arthur G. (Arthur Gregory)
Villainology : fabulous lives of the big, the bad, and
the wicked / Arthur Slade ; illustrated by Derek Mah.

ISBN 978-0-88776-809-5

1. Villains in popular culture – Juvenile fiction.   2. Villains in literature – Juvenile fiction.
3. Children's stories, Canadian (English)   I. Mah, Derek   II. Title.

PS8587.L343V45 2007   jc813'.54   C2006-905950-0

ONTARIO ARTS COUNCIL
CONSEIL DES ARTS DE L'ONTARIO

We acknowledge the financial support of the Government of Canada through
the Book Publishing Industry Development Program (BPIDP) and that of the
Government of Ontario through the Ontario Media Development Corporation's
Ontario Book Initiative.

We further acknowledge the support of the Canada Council for the Arts and the
Ontario Arts Council for our publishing program.

Printed and bound in Canada

1 2 3 4 5 6   12 11 10 09 08 07

Contents

Villains... villains all in a row...

Villains are tricky to spot! Would you recognize a villain
if you saw one? It's probably whoever is smiling the most.

The Wicked Witch of the West

———◅◉▻———

Age: Well, her skin is green, so she must be totally old. Or moldy.

Loves: Cackling, winged monkeys, the golden cap, enslaving people, umbrellas

Hates: Little dogs, girls from Kansas, water, the dark, The Witch of the North, wizards in general, Oz in particular, squirt guns

Fashion rating: C- A pointy hat? Dark, baggy clothes? That's so 1600s! C'mon, ever think of spandex?

Favorite movies: *The Witches of Eastwick*, *The Wizard of Oz* (though the ending always makes her cry), *The Lion, The Witch, and the Wardrobe*

Home: In the west where the Winkies live. Don't visit! She'll enchant you into a slave. If you decide to take your class on a field trip to her castle, just follow the setting sun. (It sets in the west, in case you were asleep in school.)

Nickname: Wih-Wih-Weh (short for Wicked Witch of the West). Also Cacklequeen, One-eye, and Greenie Meanie.

Romantic status: Single. There's no road to her castle, so she never meets anyone new.

Personality type: She has a twitchy witchy personality.

Wicked beginnings: The Wicked Witch of the West is the star of *The Wonderful Wizard of Oz*, a novel by L. Frank Baum. (The *L* stands for Lyman. Really it does – I wouldn't lie, man.) Have you read it? Have you seen the movie? You haven't! Do you live under a rock? Anyhoo, the book is all about a whiny, grouchy girl named Dorothy, and her yappy black-hearted mutt, Toto, who fly their house through a cyclone and intentionally land smack-dab on top of the Wicked Witch of the East, killing her. Do they feel remorse? Nope! In fact, Dorothy immediately steals her shoes! Murder *and* theft! Then Dorothy and her mutt gather up some brutes – a leaping lion, an ax-wielding, maniacal, tin Woodman, and a fierce, blustery scarecrow – and, following the yellow brick road, they rampage across the peaceful land of Oz. They are finally captured by the kind and beautiful Wicked Witch of the West. She treats them nicely, even tries to improve Dorothy's house-cleaning skills, but the brat splashes the Witch with water and melts her. How ungrateful. How rude!

At least this is the way the Wicked Witch told the story to me.* Dorothy may have a different version.

Ozmania: L. Frank Baum wrote fourteen books about

---

* How did the witch tell me this after she'd been melted? Well, think about it. Have you thought about it? Now think about carnivore gerbils. Funny, hey? Now what was the question?

Oz. Other authors wrote twenty-six more books. That's forty books. You could build a house with forty books! Well, a small house.

Getting an eyeful: The Wicked Witch of the West only has one eye. She lost the other one in a poker game with the Wicked Witch of the East. No big deal though. Her one eye is as powerful as a telescope and can see everywhere. Yes, she's watching you right now. Stop picking your nose. She can see that.

Bloodless: It's true. The Wicked Witch has no blood. She's so wicked it all dried up.

Invention she's waited years for: Night-vision goggles.

Water, water, everywhere: Why does the witch melt when Dorothy splashes water on her? Simple, really. She's so old that the cytoplasm (the fluid that fills each cell inside a human body) has dried up, making the nucleosis, mitochondria, nucleus, and ribosomes all rub together. The moment you add water, the cells expand so quickly that they no longer stay attached to each other, and Greenie Meanie literally falls apart and melts.

Other water facts: In the olden days, when people were stupid, they used to tie up suspected witches and throw them into a lake. If they sank and drowned, they weren't witches. If they floated, they were witches and would be weighted down with stones. It's what's called a lose/lose, drown/drown situation. That's another reason why the Wicked Witch is afraid of water.

Unbelievable accessory: In the book, the Witch carries an umbrella around wherever she goes. Of course she does!

She's afraid of water. But it's also a fashion statement. No splintery brooms for her! It makes her easy to pick out at witch conventions.

Cool cap: The Witch has a golden cap with a circle of rubies and diamonds running about it. With the cap she could summon the winged monkeys to help her. It's just like calling in the air force, except sillier. Why silly? Because to call the monkeys she had to stand on her left foot and say, "Ep-pe, pep-pe, kak-ke!" Then stand on her right foot and say, "Hil-lo, hol-lo, hel-lo!" And finally, stand on both feet and shout, "Ziz-zy, zuz-zy, zik!" Then the winged monkeys would flap in. Try it sometime. You'll feel silly too.

It's all about the shoes: In the book, the shoes are silver. But in the movie, they are ruby red. Why? In Technicolor, red stands out better on the yellow brick road than silver does. It's all about color sense!

Cool fact: Ever wonder what WWW stands for on the Internet? It stands for Wicked Witch of the West (not World Wide Web, like some people believe). The Witch runs the Internet. That's why there are so many viruses.

Pack, flock, and swarm: The witch has at her command a pack of fierce wolves, a flock of wild crows, and a swarm of black bees. She summons them all with a magic silver whistle. If you invite her to a party, ask her to leave her whistle at home.

High-school memories: The Wicked Witch attended Oz High and was teased about her long nose, gross hair, and green skin. She sat in the back of the class petting her pet bee and dreaming of the day she would crush everyone.

Interview with the Wicked Witch of the West: "Dorothy. There's a name that no one should ever call their child. All Dorothys are mean – messy and mean. Did I mention how mean they are? And no one should be allowed to have pet dogs. Especially small ones. All of them bite. If I had my way, hot dogs would be made from real dogs. I mean it. Are you listening to me? Do I have to sic my bees on you?"

Wicked Witch of the East

What do we know of this witch? Well, she made the Munchkins work night and day (so she's as bossy as your parents). She was really old, because she turned to dust as soon as Dorothy's house fell on her. And she cast a spell on the woodchopper's ax, so that it chopped him up and he had to replace his body parts with tin, becoming, you guessed it, the Tin Man. But she had one redeeming quality. Good taste in shoes.

Attila the Hun

Lived: 406 AD–453 AD

Loves: Horse riding, visiting other countries, pillaging, leering, glaring, red meat, archery

Hates: Fancy things, emperors who don't pay tribute, saddle sores, the way his gotch rides up when he's galloping

Fashion rating: C Long trousers, long-sleeved shirt, and soft riding boots – they may be comfortable for riding, but they look *sooo* plain in the palace. C'mon, Atty, spend some of your plunder! And the conic cap has *got* to go. Conic is so out this season.

Favorite saying: "Act like you own everything." Taken from his autobiography, *I Conquered the World. So There!*

Favorite movie: *Bambi*. There's something about that little, tasty deer that makes Attila's mouth water.

Nickname: The Scourge of God. This mean-sounding nickname was given to him by the Romans.

Personality type: Wandering overachiever with a conquering complex

Romantic status: Married – several times

The Huns! The Huns! The Huns were nomad tribes from North Eastern China and Central Asia. They showed up as early as 7193 BC, but weren't famous until around 375 AD (that's a long time to wait for fame). The Huns were tough, mean, and born on the backs of horses. They would fight at the drop of a bone and their main weapon was the Hun bow.

Bow to the bow: The Hun bow was a recurve bow – the special shape imparted more energy to the arrow. Simply put, the Huns could shoot farther than their enemies. If you're going to go into battle, it's always better to shoot the farthest. Try it in a balloon fight.

Attila – the early years: Attila was born around 406 AD. Doctors promptly diagnosed him with "conqueritis." He immediately took over his brother's crib, his cousin's rag toys, and the kitchen pantry. His first gifts were a pony and a bow. He was taught to ride, fire the bow, and fight in hand-to-hand combat. Oh, and he was taught to sneer.

Do judge a Hun by his cover: According to Priscus, a Greek historian, Attila was "short of stature, with a broad chest and a large head; his eyes were small, his beard thin, and sprinkled with gray; and he had a flat nose and a swarthy complexion." Not the kind of description you'd put on a dating Web site.

Number one Hun: When his uncle, Rugila, died, Attila and his brother, Bleda (cute name!), became the khans (leaders) of the Hun tribes. They invaded Persia, but lost. The brothers liked that whole invading thing though, and so they attacked the Eastern Roman Empire and only went home after the emperor admitted defeat and paid a ransom of 6,000 Roman pounds of gold. Sadly, Bleda died mysteriously in 445 AD. Some say it was a hunting accident while out with his brother ("Oops. Sorry, bro, my bow slipped."), others say in was "natural" causes (like being stabbed, trod on by a horse, or dropped off a cliff). Now Attila was the Number One Hun. He promptly invaded the Eastern Roman Empire again, then rode west, conquering what is now Austria and Germany. He was turned back by an allied Roman and Visigoth force. That didn't slow him down for long though. Next he went on a sack-and-pillage tour of Italy, then returned to his palace to plan, you guessed it, an invasion of Constantinople. But before he could carry it out, he died, and everyone in Constantinople went "Whew!" at the same time.

Attila the not-so-fun Hun: Attila did have a bad habit of killing all his enemies. In 441 AD the city of Naissus (about a hundred miles south of the Danube on the Nischava river) wouldn't yield to him, so he slaughtered every living creature inside the city walls as an example to the rest of the world. The riverbanks were covered with bones, and even years later, the stench of death was so strong no one could enter the city. *Hmmm,* I wonder where Attila's bad rep came from?

The really-not-so-fun Hun: There are rumors that Attila was a cannibal, and that he ate two of his sons. Another story is that one of his vengeful wives cooked up his sons and served them to him, saying they were wild meat. Uh, thanks, Mom! Most likely, this was just a smear campaign. As if Attila needed any more smearing.

Cool fact: Hun means "person" in Mongolian. Try that on your friends sometime. Say "You're a really, really great Hun." See if they get it.

Settling down: The Huns settled in what is now Hungary. And yes, they do get hungry once in awhile. They don't like that joke, though.

Multiple marriages: Attila loved being married. In fact, he loved it so much, he had several wives.

What's in a name? *Attila* may mean "little father" in Gothic. Or it could mean "land father" in pre-Turkish language. To the Romans *Attila* meant "Grab your togas and run!"

Now that's an empire: The empire of the Huns galloped from the steppes of Central Asia to modern Germany, and from the Danube River to the Baltic Sea.

High-school memories: When Attila went to school, he had to ride his horse uphill – both ways. He excelled in megalomania class, earning the top marks. He was also good at knitting, a little-known fact. Being Huns, the teachers conducted classes on horseback. Remember that time Attila hid snakes in his teacher's saddle? Now that was funny. What about when they played polo with that Visigoth head? A cracking good time.

Interview with Attila: "Conquering the world is really just a hobby for me. Someone has to do it. What if everyone just sat back and, well, didn't conquer? Who would get anything done? When I'm not conquering, I do like to collect coins. Lots of coins. Millions of them, in fact. Oh, and goblets and jeweled necklaces. And skulls. But I bleach the skulls before I bring them home. They don't smell as much that way."

Invention he's been waiting an eternity for: An automatic world conquest machine. It would be made of 10,000 mechanized horses and 20,000 Hun bows. But it wouldn't have any horse offal ("poop," for those who don't know what *offal* is).

Nothing fancy, please: Attila ate off a wooden platter and drank from a wooden goblet. Guess he didn't mind slivers. He did let his guests eat from silver platters and goblets. Very classy of him.

Attila's untimely end: Attila died on his wedding night. Oops. He drank too much alcohol, got what was believed to be the worst nosebleed ever, choked on his own blood, and left this world. That's so amazingly gross! His funeral party was killed to keep his burial place secret. Nice funeral!

The Wolf

Age: 15 dog years old (a coon's age)

Loves: Huffing, puffing, pork, kid flesh (as in baby goat), wearing sheep's clothing, talking to his food before he eats it, mutton

Hates: Brick houses, huntsmen, smart pigs, chimneys, boys who cry wolf (and mean it), nosy little girls in red

Fashion rating: *B*+ Fur is in this year, especially if it's attached to the owner and well groomed. He should get a manicure.

Favorite sayings: "Little pig, little pig, let me come in," and "The better to eat you with."

Favorite movies: *Babe, Animal Farm, Never Cry Wolf*

Least favorite movie: *Who's Afraid of Virginia Woolf?* (He thought there'd be at least one wolf. And maybe a pig. Instead: a lot of humans talking.) *Dancing with Wolves* was another big letdown. There wasn't even a cha-cha!

Nicknames: *Canis lupus badus*, Mr. Big, Mr. Bad, Wolfie, Mr. Huff, Mr. Puff, Mr. Blow-The-House-Down

Personality type: Chatty carnivore

Romantic status: Single. He's kind of a lone wolf.

The totally toothfull origin: The Wolf guest stars in several fairytales, the most popular ones are "Three Little Pigs" and "Little Red Riding Hood." In the pig story, he huffs down two houses, eats two pigs, and finally tries to blow over the brick house, but he runs out of puff. So he climbs down the chimney and is boiled in a pot of water. The pig eats him. Ha! A pig-eating a wolf. Now if that's not worth a giggle, what is? In the other tale, the wolf swallows a grandma, then dresses up in her clothes and tricks her cute red-riding-hooded granddaughter into coming close enough to also be swallowed whole. A huntsman drops by and slices The Wolf open, saving the humans. Then they stitch stones in The Wolf's stomach and he tries to run away, but dies (proof that stones in your stomach are bad for you). It's always a bad ending for The Wolf. He might as well hang out with Humpty Dumpty.

F is for fables: Fables are stories with a moral at the end. The Wolf is incredibly popular in these fables. The best known is *The Boy Who Cried Wolf*. In this story, a nerdy shepherd boy cries out "Wolf! Wolf! Help, or it will kill my sheep!" just to get the villagers running. He thinks he's being funny. Except when the real wolf arrives he cries wolf and no one comes so Wolfie eats all his sheep. Stupid shepherd boy! Doesn't he know that lying never pays? (That's the moral of the story.)

Favorite pastime: Dressing up as someone else. He'll wear Grandma's clothes or sheep's clothing, which is really its fleece. (He fleeced it, get it?) He once dressed up as a principal, but no one noticed the difference.

The Real Wolf

Wolves have been howling across this earth for about a million years (since the Pleistocene Age). Most are known as *canis lupus* (gray wolves) and they have a habit of hunting in packs and eating sheep (and other herbivores). This puts them on the bad side of farmers and thus, when people tell stories, the wolf is almost always the villain. Oddly enough, many humans have wolves in their homes (the family dog is directly descended from wolves).

The big, good wolf: Not all stories have wolves as sneering, evil carnivores. In Native American mythology the wolf is portrayed as brave, full of honor (not full of children or grandmas), and intelligent. According to Roman mythology, Romulus and Remus, two warriors, were raised by a female wolf (actually they were nursed by the wolf, but that's too gross to mention). The two men went on to found Rome, the city that gave us the Roman Empire. So where would the Roman Empire be without that wolf, hey?

Cool wolf game: A British game is called *What's the Time, Mr. Wolf?* It begins with one child standing with his back to several children. The other kids call out "What's the time, Mr. Wolf?" and he answers "It's ten o'clock!" And the children all have to take ten steps toward the wolf. They repeat the question and he answers. Then when they get close enough and someone asks "What's the time, Mr. Wolf?" he yells "Dinner time!" and runs after the children. Whoever he catches becomes the wolf. Don't play this with a real wolf.

How to know if you're dating The Wolf: Does your boyfriend dress up in your grandmother's clothes? Dump him! He's either The Wolf, or he's really, really weird.

High-school memories: The Wolf went to a brick schoolhouse on the corner of the woods and was in the same grade as Red Riding Hood and the four little pigs. *Four* little pigs, you ask? I thought there were three. Well, read on, dear curious reader. Wolfie sat in the back, salivating and answering questions with a howl. After eating one of the pigs, he was sent to reform school, where they taught him to hold his breath whenever he got angry. That's how he learned to huff and puff.

Interview with The Wolf: "I'm so depressed. The doctor says all the pork I eat is bad for my heart. I know I've put on a little weight, but really! It's my job! It's a wolf-eat-pig world out there. If I didn't eat pigs, they'd be building straw and stick houses everywhere. Do you want pigs living in your neighborhood? They put the sty in pigsty and they wallow in mud! Mud! The other thing that the doc is worried about is my habit of swallowing my prey whole. All their kicking and struggling while they digest is hard on my stomach. And my spleen! I have to remember to chew at least twelve or thirteen times before I swallow. And the huffing and puffing – that's my asthma. The puffer has helped clear that up, though."

Invention he's been waiting an eternity for: An automatic pig catcher.

Another famous wolf: Fenrir, is the biggest and the baddest of all the wolves. He appears in old norse Mythology (that's the stories of the Vikings). He's the son of Loki, the trickster god, and Angrboda, a giantess. He starts out small, but soon grows so large that the gods have to bind him with a special rope. He gets angry and bites off the hand of Tyr (a god). Then, when the world is about to end, Fenrir breaks his rope and swallows Odin, the king of all the gods, whole. Fenrir is later killed by Odin's son, Vidar. See, it's always a bad ending for The Wolf. Why not a happy ending where the wolf retires to a land full of sheep and slow-moving pigs?

Billy the Kid

Birthplace: Maybe New York City, maybe Indiana

Birthdate: 1859 or 1860 or 1861 (He didn't have a birth certificate.)

Deathdate: July 14, 1881 (shot through the heart by good ol' sheriff Pat Garrett)

Loves: Gunslinging, cow rustling, poker, polkas, square dancing (considered cool back then), target shooting, people shooting

Hates: Sheriffs, deputies, jails, handcuffs

Fashion rating: *A-* Unshaven face, weather-beaten sugar-loaf sombrero with a wide ornamental band, smelling of gunsmoke. Hey! Western style is back in.

Eyes: Sky blue

Height: Five feet, eight inches

Hair: Sandy blond and prone to cowboy-hat-head

Personality type: Romantic murderer

Romantic status: Single

Real name: William Henry McCarty

Nicknames and aliases: Billy the Kid, Kid Antrim, William H. Bonney

Favorite song: Turkey in the straw. It had lyrics like: *Went out to milk, and I didn't know how/I milked the goat instead of the cow.* Ho, ho! Okay, so they didn't have any good music back then.

Favorite movies: *Billy the Kid, Billy the Kid vs. Dracula, Young Guns*

Nickname game: William was nicknamed Billy the Kid by J.H. Koogler, the editor of the *Las Vegas Gazette*. In an article he said: "The gang is under the leadership of 'Billy the Kid,' a desperate cuss, who is eligible for the post of captain of any crowd, no matter how mean or lawless." Cuss! He used the word cuss! How vulgar.

Favorite firearms: Billy *loved* his Colt Single Action .44 and Colt Double Action .41 caliber six-shooter (called The Thunderer), but his favorite gun was his Winchester 73 rifle.

Cool fact: Billy could take a revolver in each hand and twirl them in different directions at the same time. Don't try this at home!

Outlaw origin: Billy's dad died either before Billy was born, or shortly after. His mother eventually moved to Silver City, New Mexico and re-married, then died from tuberculosis (note to self, don't live in the Wild, Wild West – it's yucky). Billy was fourteen at the time. He made a good impression on folks but was arrested and jailed for hiding a bundle of clothes, helping to play a prank on a Chinese laundryman. Billy wormed his way out up the jailhouse chimney. (I guess you could say he got sooted up.) He found work hauling logs, until he had an argument with a bullying blacksmith, which ended up with Billy shooting the blacksmith. The man died and Billy was placed in the guardhouse, but he escaped. He went to Arizona, then New Mexico, where he worked for a rancher. When his boss was shot by a deputy, Billy vowed revenge and gunned down the deputy, the sheriff, and another deputy (note to self, don't get Billy mad). The Kid was promised amnesty if he would testify against some other outlaws. He agreed, and was put in jail. Oops. Did we forget about the amnesty? No problem. Billy slipped out of his handcuffs and escaped, yet again. He turned to cattle rustling and theft, and was now almost always referred to as Billy the Kid. He was captured in an abandoned stone building and jailed. Guess what happened next. He escaped! This time a friend had hidden guns in the outhouse (privvy is the fancy name). Billy used them to shoot his two guards. He fled, but Sheriff Pat Garrett hunted him down and shot him twice. Billy was buried the next day at Fort Sumner's Cemetery. Jeepers – it sounds like fun, except for all the shooting and dying and square dancing.

Famous last words: Billy's last words were, "*¿Quien es? ¿Quien es?*" which is Spanish for "Who is it? Who is it?" You see, Billy had just entered a darkened room, not knowing the sheriff was hiding there, ready to gun him down.

Twenty-one men gunned down: Billy was said to have killed twenty-one men before he turned twenty-one – one for each year of his life. Truth is, he shot four and killed five with the help of other outlaws. And he never made it to his twenty-first birthday.

High-school memories: Billy's high school days were spent in a cattle rustlin' school. They taught roping, hiding in gullies, and gun twirling. Billy excelled at everything, except mustache growing.

Interview with Billy the Kid: "Stealing stock, gambling, horse theft, and shooting sheriffs. Sure I've done those things, but I was having a bad day – maybe two. What have I done wrong lately? That's the real question. All I've done today is eat my grub and shoot a few bottles. Oh, and a deputy. But he had it comin'. Have you seen me twirl my guns?"

How to know if you're dating Billy the Kid: Are your father's cattle missing? Is your date always looking over his shoulder? You're dating Billy the Kid.

Other Dastardly Outlaws

Ned Kelly: This Aussie bush ranger rustled cattle, killed a few constables, and robbed two banks, along with the help of his gang. On June 28, 1880, the gang dressed in armor and had a shoot-out with police. The armor didn't cover their legs, so they all got shot in the legs and fell down. Ned was hanged later, his last words being, "Ah well, I suppose it has come to this . . . Such is life." What a philosopher!

Song Jiang: This Chinese "Billy the Kid" did his outlawing back in the twelfth century, in Shandong and Henan provinces. He and his army of bandits robbed people on the roads and up and down the Huai River Valley. Song Jiang decided they weren't getting enough action, so they went to the coast, boarded ten huge ships, and invaded a nearby city. A thousand-man army met them, burned their ships, and captured Song Jiang. It was his swan song, so to speak.

Robin Hood: Yep, he's the guy in dashing green, who stole from the rich and gave to the poor. Robin was an English folk hero banished from his own lands by the Sheriff of Nottingham, and forced to become an outlaw. Those darn bad sheriffs were even around in the 1190s!

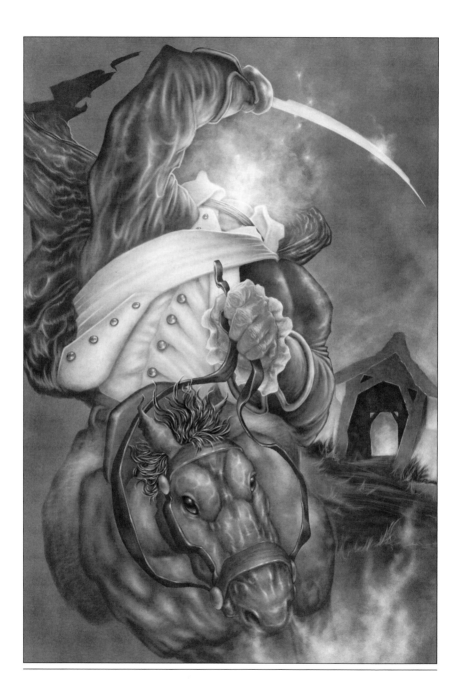

The Headless Horseman

Age: Dead

Loves: Night riding, Halloween, how people's eyeballs get big when he rides by, the witching hour, how he never hits his head on branches

Hates: Trying to brush his teeth, when his head itches, cannonballs, people who don't believe he's real

Fashion rating: B+ Only he could make "going headless" fashionable. Eighteenth century military uniform! Spurs! And a black steed. What could be cooler?

Hairstyle: No one knows

Favorite saying: "Always think ahead." Get it? A head. See, he has no head and so that's funny. Hey, he knocked 'em dead with this joke at the Guillotine Convention.

Favorite movies: *The Adventures of Ichabod and Mr. Toad, Sleepy Hollow, King Henry the VIII*

Favorite haunts: Sleepy Hollow, adjacent roads, and the graveyard

Nickname: Headless Hessian of the Hollow

Hey, where did my head go? The Hessian horseman apparently lost his wits . . . and his head . . . when a cannon-ball decapitated him during some nameless battle of the American Revolution.

Hey, Hessian! A *Hessian* is a "German mercenary" who served in the British Forces during the American revolution. Apparently Hessians were good riders, but no one taught them how to duck.

His nightly habit: Every night Mr. Headless rises up from his churchyard grave, mounts his horse, and gallops to the scene of the battle where he lost his head, like a golf player looking for a lost ball. Just before the sun rises he rides hard, like a midnight blast, because he has to get back to his grave before daybreak. Actually, come to think of it, being the headless horseman would be really, really boring.

The legend: So the year is 1787-ish and this skinny, tall Ichabod teacher guy comes to Sleepy Hollow to be the schoolmaster. He goes all googly-eyed for the hottest girl in town, Katrina Van Tassel. (Now that's a name!) But Abraham "Brom Bones" Van Brunt is also after her hand (and the rest of her). Who'll win? Grasshopper-limbs Ichabod, or the muscleman with the square jaw? One night, both of them try to woo her at a dance. First Ichabod dances with her, and surprise, he's a great dancer! Brom Bones entertains her by telling ghost stories, including the story of the Headless Horseman. When Ichabod rides home that night all he can think of are the ghost stories. The Horseman appears, chases

Ichabod, then throws his head at the teacher. (Don't try this at school.) In the morning Ichabod's horse is found at his home, but the teacher has disappeared. The only evidence of his encounter with the ghost is a smashed pumpkin and the schoolmaster's hat. Spooky.

Head-throwing contest: When he does finally find his head, he throws it at Ichabod. That's no way to treat your own head!

Have you ever wondered . . . Whether anyone made pumpkin pie out of the inside of the Horseman's head? Or would that be brain pie? *Hmmmm.*

Personality type: Thinker. Well he was before that whole "headless" incident.

Romantic status: Single. Though he did briefly date the ghost of Marie Antoinette.

High-school memories: High school was a grand time for the Hessian. He had a marvelous head of hair, which he combed every day. Girls swooned with love every time he strode by. Now they swoon in fear. Oddly enough, he was voted "most likely to have pumpkin for brains."

Interview with a Headless Hessian: "That whole American Revolution thing, I thought it was going to be groovy, cool, and fun: a nice trip across to the New Continent, maybe a skirmish or two, and some surfing. Instead, cannons to the left, cannons to the right, and well, obviously more cannons than I could keep track of. Do you know what it's like having your head knocked off by a cannonball? It stings! What can I say, I was having a bad head day."

Invention he's been waiting an eternity for: A hand-held GPS-HF (Global Positioning System Head Finder).
How to know if you're dating the Headless Horseman: When you kiss him, does it feel like you're kissing air?
Medical note: Losing your head can be bad for your health.

Other Headless Haunters

The Headless Ship Captain: In St. John's, Newfoundland, there was a sea captain who loved spending time with a beautiful local lady. Unfortunately, her landlubber boyfriend got jealous. Then he got busy sharpening his sword. One night, the jealous lover snuck up to the captain and lopped off his head. He was never convicted, so the ghost is still searching for both his head and his murderer.

Anne Boleyn: She was Henry VIII's second wife. Well, until he had her beheaded, that is. She now spends her evenings walking the corridors of the Tower of London, headless. She has to be careful, though. There are lots of headless ghosts at the Tower, including Henry's fifth wife. It's always kind of awkward when they bump into each other.

Morgan le Fay

Age: 32

Occupation: Enchantress (a classy way of saying witch), sorceress (a cool way of saying witch), priestess, plotress

Home: Gore. Really, it was a place called Gore. That's what she gets for being married to King Urien of Gore.

Loves: Plotting, stealing Excalibur, switching the *n* and the *e* in her husband's last name

Hates: When her plans are foiled, Arthur, Guinevere

Fashion rating: *A+* She's got that whole "I'm a sorceress, look at me" thing worked out. And she has ultra-mysterious eyes and ravishing red hair. She sets the Camelot walkway on fire (literally)!

Hairstyle: Flowing, wild and yet controlled – her hair is her best feature. She uses a spell to hold it in place. (They didn't have styling gel back then.)

Romantic Status: Married, most of the time (though she does try to kill her husband).

Nicknames: Morgaine, Morgain, Morgana, Morgie-poo (Actually only King Uriens could call her this.)

Favorite saying: "Whatsoever come of me, my brother shall not have this scabbard." She said this just before throwing Excalibur's magical scabbard into the lake. Kind of sums up her attitude to King Arthur. She didn't want him to have anything.

Favorite movies: *Excalibur, Camelot, Monty Python and the Holy Grail, The Sword in the Stone*

Arthurian origin: Morgan le Fay is the half sister of King Arthur (the star of all those Arthurian stories where he pulls the sword Excalibur from a stone, unites the kingdom, then sits around a round table). Morgan doesn't much like her bro, though. First he gives her Excalibur for safekeeping. She instantly makes a duplicate and gives that back to Arthur. She hands the real sword to Accolan, her lover, who fights Arthur in single combat, wounds him, but drops the sword. Arthur picks it up, wins the fight, and Accolan dies. Hey, great plan, Morgan! While the king is recovering from his wounds, she steals Excalibur's protective scabbard and rides away with forty horsemen. Arthur chases after her, but she throws the scabbard into a lake then runs into a valley and turns herself and her companions into stones. Very clever trick! Next she has a maiden deliver a lovely mantle to her brother, asking to be forgiven. He is about to put the jeweled cloak on when the Lady of the Lake says, "Uh, Artie, maybe you shouldn't wear it until the woman who brought it has tried it on." He agrees and the maiden slips it on and is burned to a cinder. Foiled again! Later Morgan sends a drinking horn to Camelot that no unfaithful lady can drink out of without spilling. Guinevere drinks from it and spills. Ooops! Turns out she is having an affair with Lancelot. What a soap opera! Anyway, Morgan retires to her Castle of Tauroc and everyone assumes she is dead. But one day while out hunting, Arthur comes across her and says, "Gee, sis, you're forgiven for trying to kill me and for wrecking my marriage and my kingdom." To which Morgan replies, "Yeah, sorry about that. I won't do it again." Much later, after Arthur is wounded in the final battle against his son Mordred, Morgan is one of the four women who take Arthur to the island of Avalon to be healed. Now she's a nurse? Guess she threw away her Villainess Club Points card and gave up her wicked ways.

Cool fact: *Fay* means a "fairy" or an "elf."

Other origin: Some very wise scholars think Morgan is descended from Modron, a mother goddess of Celtic myth, or from the Morganes, a group of Breton water fairies.

Cool facts: A *fata morgana* is a "mirage" in the Strait of Messina. It's the result of temperature inversion, which makes things on the horizon (ships or cliffs) look long and elevated, like fairy-tale castles.

High-school memories: Morgan loved potion class. Her favorite potion was the *loof gnicnad erauqs* potion. Its ingredients included eye of newt, toe of frog, wool of bat, and tongue of dog. Oh, and a whole lot of chili peppers. What did the potion do? It turned the drinker into a square dancer. It was *sooooo* hilarious when she snuck it into the punch at the teachers' staff meeting. Why was it called loof gnicnad erauqs? You figure it out.

Interview with Morgan le Fay: "So, like Artie got everything – the best horse, the nicest blankets, oh, and the throne. Talk about spoiled! Okay, so he was raised as a pauper by Merlin, but at least he didn't have to grow up in a nunnery!"

How to know if you're dating Morgan le Fay: Does she keep complaining about her brother, the king? Is she trying to get you to challenge him to a duel? She's Morgan le Fay. Dump her gently. She knows how to get revenge.

Other Arthurian Villains

Mordred: He was Arthur's son or nephew, depending on which story you believe. Either way, he put the dread in Mordred. He once came to Arthur's court and devoured all the food and drink. Can you imagine the belch! When Arthur was off fighting Rome he left Mordred in charge. Mordred made himself king and married Guinevere! Arthur returned and a great battle was fought at Camlann, which resulted in Mordred's death and in Arthur's fatal wound. Next time don't leave the kingdom in Mordred's hands, okay? And don't give him the keys to the car, either.

La belle dame sans merci: She was a banshee (a female spirit in Gaelic folklore) who lived in the enchanted forest (just past the unenchanted forest, over the ogre bridge). Her name means "The beautiful lady without mercy." She attracted knights and made them fall so hopelessly in love that they couldn't move or do anything but think about her. Nice hobby.

Nimue: The enchantress who enchanted Merlin and imprisoned him in a tree. Forever. That meant Arthur couldn't call him up for advice. Even if he knocked on his tree. Odd thing is, Nimue was also the Lady of the Lake, who gave Arthur his sword and saved him several times. Doesn't anyone make sense in these stories?

Qin Hui

Age: Born 1090, died 1155
Occupation: Chief counselor to the Southern Song emperor, Gaozong
Home: China
Loves: Plotting, giving up parts of China to the enemy, fibbing
Hates: Generals, the way people think of him these days, deep-fried dough, being cast in iron
Fashion rating: *B* Nice courtly robes and a perfect manicure. Sadly, the sneer gives away his inner-traitor.
Personality type: Officious court official
Birthplace: Jiangning, Jiangsu Province, China
Hairstyle: He wore his hair Tang Dynasty style! Ha! It was the Song Dynasty! You're a dynasty behind, Qin Hui!
Romantic status: Married – to an equally treacherous wife
Favorite saying: *"Mo xu you."* When people in modern-day China use this phrase, they are describing a trumped-up charge.

Favorite movies: They didn't have movies back then, silly. He did have a few favorite Chinese operas, though. To Qin Hui, the best operas were the ones with a really, really interesting villain.

The story of Qin Hui: Qin Hui is to China, what Benedict Arnold is to America. First off, way back in 907 AD, the Tang Dynasty toppled and China was plunged into years of darkness. Finally a general, Sung Taizu, became emperor in 960, and things went along swell until the 1120s. That's when the Jin (people from Northern China) invaded central China. In fact, they eventually seized the capital and took the emperor prisoner. A new emperor was chosen and he sent a brave general, Yue Fei, to lead his army against the Jins. Yue Fei won victory after victory, reclaiming lost territory. But just when it looked like he had the Jin on the run, Yue Fei was called back to the emperor's court and removed from duty. Why? The new emperor was worried that if Yue Fei beat the Jin, the old emperor would be released and he would be out of a job. Then Mr. Plotter himself, Qin Hui, stepped in and accused Yue Fei of a terrible crime and the general was executed. When another general asked what crime Yue Fei had committed, Qin Hui answered, "*Mo xu you*," which meant "Something fairly likely." In other words, the charges were made up. As if that wasn't bad enough, Qin Hui helped convince the emperor to relinquish Northern China to the Jin so that there could be peace. He gave away half of China, just like that! The good news is that the Song dynasty eventually beat the Jin. The bad news is in order to do it they allied themselves with Genghis Khan and his not-so-friendly Mongols. The Mongols decided to take China for their own. And that was the end of the Song dynasty.

A little more about the general: General Yue Fei had the characters for *absolute devotion to the nation* tattooed to his back. It's not wise to execute a general who is that dedicated. He is still an extremely popular hero in China.

Infamy in iron forever: Years later, General Yue Fei was cleared of all charges and a temple was built in his honor. Before his tomb kneel four cast iron statues – Qin Hui, his wife, and two lackeys. People still visit the tomb today to curse and spit on them.

High-school memories: Qin spent a lot of his high school in the principal's office. He wasn't in trouble, he was just ratting on everyone else. He was often bothered by bullies, but he found if he gave them his lunch, they'd go away. He assumed the same would happen when he later gave up Northern China.

Interview with Qin Hui: "Listen, it's a lot of work being a court official. There are papers to sign and bums to kiss. Oh, and I have to do my hair every day. What would a simple general know about the intricacies of court life? If we got the old emperor back, I'd be looking for new work. Nah, things are better this way, believe you me. Who's gonna miss one little general and a bit of second-rate land to the north?"

Interesting, but fattening fact: After Yue Fei was executed, a pastry chef twisted two pastry shapes together, calling them Qin Hui and his wife. He then put the dough in boiling oil, and people came from miles around to take bites out of the deep-fried Qin Hui. It is said to be the origin of *Youtiao*, a common breakfast food in China.

Other Traitors

Benedict Arnold: He was an American general during the American Revolutionary War who plotted to surrender a fort to the British at West Point, New York. That plotting! It's so hard to do! Arnold wrote his plot out on papers for the British and gave them to a spy to carry. The spy hid them in his boot! Unfortunately, that's the first place the Americans looked when they caught him. Arnold's plans discovered, he fled to the British on a frigate named *Vulture*. Symbolic name, eh?

Brutus: Ah, good ol' Brutus. He was a Roman senator who had fought against Julius Caesar, but Caesar pardoned him and made him governor of Gaul. But when the rest of the senators decided to assassinate Caesar, Brutus was right beside them with his knife out. To which Caesar said in Latin: "*Tu quoque, Brute, fili mihi?*" It means, "You too, Brutus, my son?" He could also have said, "Thanks for nothing, Brute!"

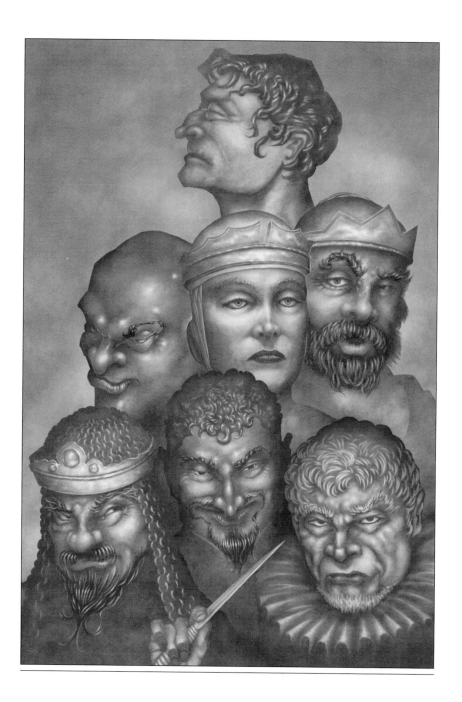

Shakespearian Villains

William Shakespeare (April 26, 1564–April 23, 1616) was an English poet and playwright who couldn't seem to write anything that didn't rhyme. He is the Godzilla of English literature. He stomps on all competition for biggest and best writer (in English), ever. His plays were amazingly successful and were even performed before Queen Elizabeth I. Good ol' Will gave us some absolutely darling little villains.

Iago: He is the villain of the play *Othello*, and perhaps the worst of the worst. Iago is the supposed best friend of Othello, except Iago is jealous of everything Othello has – good looks, a fine reputation, a happy (and brand-new) marriage. So Iago first convinces Othello that his wife is untrue (Othello murders her) then Iago destroys Othello's reputation and Othello stabs himself and dies. But Iago's wife tells everyone how bad Iago has been and he's imprisoned. Poor, poor Iago. Who will you plot against now?

Richard III: What's so bad about Richard the III from the play *Richard the III*? For one thing, he says, "I am determined to prove a villain." And boy does he. First he bumps off his older brother so he can be next in line for the throne. When his oldest brother, the king, dies, Richard assumes control. Heads fly – including his two young nephews'. Rebels and an invading earl put an end to ol' Richie, who is unhorsed in the final battle and cries, "A horse! A horse! My kingdom for a horse!" He doesn't get a horse – instead, he used as a living pincushion until he dies!

Richard III's favorite saying: "Conscience is but a word that cowards use, devised at first to keep the strong in awe." In other words, he has no conscience.

Macbeth: This is a play about nagging and ambition. Macbeth, a Scottish guy, is told by three witches that he's going to become king. His wife, Lady Macbeth, nags him until he bumps off Duncan, the king. Macbeth becomes king, and his wife goes mad with guilt. Finally, Macbeth is captured and beheaded. See, being ambitious doesn't always pay off.

Macbeth plots murder: "Stars, hide your fires; Let not light see my black and deep desires: The eye wink at the hand; yet let that be, Which the eye fears, when it is done, to see." He's plotting murder, but wants to close his eyes while he does it. Just buy sunglasses, Macbeth.

Lady Macbeth: She's Macbeth's wife, who nags, cajoles, hints, and pushes her husband into murdering the king. She plans it all out and even plots a few more murders, but her conscience catches up with her and she begins to sleepwalk, shouting out her guilt. She dies (by her own hand), or she is claimed by demons. Shakespeare leaves that up in the air.

No, she's not yelling at the dog: "Out, damned spot! out, I say!" Here Lady Macbeth has gone mad, is sleepwalking, and trying to wash invisible bloodstains from her hands. Either that, or it's a sixteenth-century product placement – a laundry commercial in the middle of Macbeth.

A funny thing about *Macbeth*: The play is considered unlucky by actors. They call it "the Scottish play" because they believe it's bad luck to say the play's name inside a theater. Maybe they should just get lucky socks.

Gaius Cassius: Cassius is a jealous senator who thinks that Julius Caesar is going to turn Rome into a monarchy and rule as king. Even Caesar notices his "hungry" eyes when he says, "Yond Cassius has a lean and hungry look. He thinks too much; such men are dangerous." Cassius convinces all the senators, especially Brutus (a friend of Caesar), to have a stabbing party, with Caesar as the guest of honor. After they poke several holes into Caesar, a civil war erupts and Cassius and Brutus are defeated in battle. They fall on their own swords instead of surrendering. Nice plan, Cassius!

His motto: "The fault, dear Brutus, is not in our stars, But in ourselves, that we are underlings." (We could be more if we just tried harder.) Sounds great, except that by "trying harder" he means they should stab Caesar.

Aaron the Moor: Aaron is a villain from the tragedy *Titus Andronicus*. It is the bloodiest and grossest Shakespearian play. Eye-poppingly gross! Heads, hands, even tongues roll in this one. I can't tell you all the things that happen, but I will point out that Aaron is the servant to Tamora, the queen of the Goths (no, she didn't wear black and bang her head), and he's amazingly bad. He's captured by the Romans and buried chest-deep and left to starve.

His final words: "If one good deed in all my life I did, I do repent it from my very soul." He really is a villain.

The Duke of Cornwall: Cornwall is a conniving, plotting, heartless star of King Lear. In this play, King Lear abdicates, planning to leave his kingdom to his three daughters, but surprise, surprise! Several battles, poisonings, and hair-pullings occur. Cornwall, the husband of one daughter, jumps into the fray. He puts an earl in the stocks, leaves King Lear out in the open during a storm, and gouges out the Earl of Gloucester's eyes. Cornwall's planning and plotting end when Gloucester's servant attacks him and mortally wounds him. (It's all documented on the reality TV show *When Servants Attack!!*)

Getting an eyeful: "Out, vile jelly!" This is what Cornwall says as he, uh, plops out Gloucester's eye. Now that's good writing!

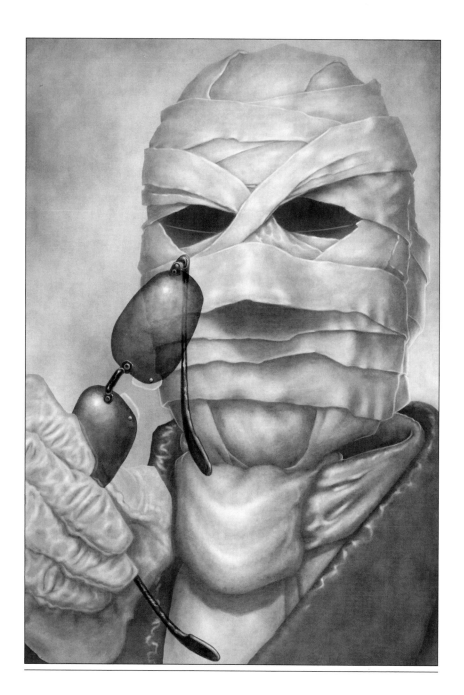

The Invisible Man

Age: Early 30s

Real Name: Griffin

Loves: Tapping people on the back, tripping people, eavesdropping, talking to himself, smashing plates, planning out world domination

Hates: Snoopy villagers, bloodhounds, snow, when he argues with himself, watching his food digest

Fashion rating: F- He's invisible and he's naked. Gross!

Home: Jolly ol' England

Favorite haunts: Port Burdock, England. Wow, he's invisible and he can go anywhere in the world and he chooses Port Burdock. Why not someplace warm? You're not wearing any clothes, silly. GO SOMEPLACE WARM!

Favorite saying: "Yoo-hoo! Over here! Right here!"

Personality type: Opaque and selfish. He tends to only think about what's good for the Invisible Man.

Hairstyle: Who knows?

Abilities: Sneaking, stalking, spying, eavesdropping

Romantic Status: Single. He did set up a date with the Invisible Woman, but they couldn't find each other.

His most crazy statement: "Port Burdock is no longer under the queen, tell your Colonel of Police, and the rest of them; it is under me – the Terror! This is day one of year one of the new epoch – the Epoch of the Invisible Man. I am Invisible Man the First!" Uh, I think he's going a little batty.

Cool fact: Griffin first experimented on a cat, turning it invisible. It's the one you hear, but never see, at night in the back alley.

Cool fact2: His blood becomes visible as it coagulates. Apparently only living material can stay invisible. It's a well-known fact in scientific circles.

Invisible origin: H.G. Wells was a Brit writer who gave us such works as *The War of the Worlds* and *The Time Machine.* In 1897 he wrote *The Invisible Man.* In the story, Griffin was a young albino scientist who invented a marvelous formula that bent light and turned the body invisible. (It's obvious when you think about it.) Like all crazy scientists, he tried it out on himself. It worked. He was invisible! But he forgot to make a formula to make himself visible again. Ooops!! In order to fit in with society, he would wrap himself in bandages and wear a mask and glasses. It worked great until he had to eat, which meant he always ate by himself. Eventually, Griffin decided he must find a way of turning visible and he got a room at an inn. In order to pay his rent, he burgled. Soon the police were hot on his trail. Did I mention the formula had a side effect? Griffin was starting to turn into a mad scientist. And I mean crazy-mad *and* mad-mad. First he gave his money to a tramp to carry, but then the tramp carried it away. Griffin followed him to Port Burdock. He found a schoolmate, Arthur Kemp, whom he invited to be his visible partner, so they could start a reign of terror and take over Port Burdock. Wow, talk about thinking small. Kemp called the cops and Griffin planned to murder Kemp as an example, but in the end, the people of Port Burdock all came out and mobbed the invisible man to death. His invisibility formula wore off, bit by bit. First they could see veins, then arteries, nerves, bones, and skin. Finally, he was all there in his nakedness. Gross!

Another visibly odd quote: "I could be invisible! To do such a thing would be to transcend magic. And I beheld, unclouded by doubt, a magnificent vision of all that invisibility might mean to a man – the mystery, the power, the freedom. Drawbacks I saw none."

High-school memories: High school was the greatest time of the Invisible Man's life. He played defense for the football team and scored a sack nearly every play. He put tacks on the teachers' chairs and was never caught. (Don't try this at your school.) He could skip class without anyone noticing. Sadly, he was a great dancer, but no one ever saw his moves.

Interview with the Invisible Man: "I thought being invisible would be such a gas! Playing pranks! Eavesdropping!

Free movies! But hey, try riding the bus and have some six-foot biker sit on you. Ouch! And don't think of using the pedestrian crosswalk. I've been hit by cars three times. Dental work; I don't even want to talk about that. And what's the point of taking over the world if no one can see you? They won't know when the right time to bow is. Bah! Invisibility isn't all it's cracked up to be."

Invention he's been waiting a lifetime for: A de-invisibility potion

How to know if you're dating the Invisible Man: Does your doorbell ring and there's no one there? Does the car seem to be driving itself? Can you see the popcorn being chewed and digested in a stomach? You're dating the Invisible Man.

What isn't explained: Okay, let's say you can turn the body invisible by making it so that it doesn't absorb or reflect light. How does the Invisible Man see? The eyes must absorb some light to see. Put that in your pipe and smoke it, H.G. Wells.

Medical note: Being invisible doesn't cure pimples, but at least no one can see them.

Favorite movies: *The Invisible Man, The Invisible Man Returns, The Invisible Woman, Hollow Man*

Invisible on film: In the 1933 classic movie, when the Invisible Man takes off his bandages, the special effects team made the actor appear invisible by dressing him in black

velvet and filming him in front of a black velvet background.
Clever!

Invisible death on film: In the 1933 movie, the Invisible
Man is betrayed by his footsteps in the snow. The police
shoot him. Those police, they always get their man.

Emperor Nero

Birthdate: December 15, 37 AD

Deathdate: June 9, 68 AD

Age: 31

Occupation: Emperor of the Roman Empire, part-time lounge act

Hobbies include: Acting, singing, charioteering, and lyre playing. Oh, and poisoning.

Home: Rome, capital of the Roman Empire

Other names: Okay, try to stick with me on this one: Nero was born with the name Lucius Domitius Ahenobarbus, but when he was adopted by Claudius, the then Roman Emperor, Lucius changed his name to Nero Claudius Drusus Germanicus. When Claudius died, Nero called himself Nero Claudius Caesar Augustus Germanicus. Oh, as if that wasn't enough, in 66 AD he added the prefix *Imperator* to his name (it means "commander-in-chief"), making him Imperator Nero Claudius Caesar Augustus Germanicus. Those Romans! No wonder they won so many battles. Their enemies thought they were being attacked by twenty emperors, not just one.

Loves: Singing to captive audiences, poisoning his enemies, pyromania

Hates: How everyone always plots against him, that whole "look after the empire" thing, when Christians whine about being thrown to the lions

Fashion rating: *C* Nero had fair hair, odd blue eyes, a fat neck, a pot belly, and he smelled bad (not entirely his fault, they didn't have Old Spice back then). Oh, and he had spots. Lots of 'em. He often wore a dressing gown, but no belt (now that's a major fashion faux pas), no shoes and a scarf around his neck. An emperor with a scarf! No shoes on his smelly feet! He wouldn't even get served in most restaurants today.

Personality type: Imperialistic and impish

Birthplace: Antium (It's called Anzio, now, though. And it's in Italy.)

Romantic status: Married twice. Neither wife survived the relationship.

Nicknames: Nero the Zero, the Fickle Fiddler, the Beast, Mr. Party, Lyre, Lyre, Pants on Fire

Favorite movies: *Ben Hur*, *Gladiator*, *Spartacus*, *Towering Inferno*, *Fiddler on the Roof*

Nero's not-so-pretty history: When Nero was two, his mother, Agrippina, was banished by Emperor Caligula (apparently for helping to plot his downfall). Then Nero's father died, and Nero's inheritance was confiscated. Already, his life was looking lumpy. Things got brighter when Caligula was murdered and the new emperor, Claudius, recalled

Agrippina from banishment. She had re-married, but sadly, her husband died of poisoning. So she married Emperor Claudius, who promptly adopted Nero, making him his heir apparent. He even gave Nero his very own tutor, Seneca. (Wow! Imagine having one teacher following you around all the time!) Sadly, Claudius died. (Poison again. It seems Agrippina was always mixing the salt shaker up with the poison shaker.) Nero, now seventeen, became the youngest emperor yet. Mommy helped him run things, though, along with his tutor. The first five years of his rein were the best ever for the Roman Empire! But, Nero got tired of Mommy always telling him what to do, so he pushed her aside, and she began supporting his stepbrother, Brittanicus, to be emperor. Sadly, Brittanicus died of poisoning. (Nero had learned a lot from his mom.) Nero decided to get rid of her, too, so he tried to poison her — three times. Then he rigged the ceiling above her bed to fall on her. It missed, so he sent her on a leaky boat that sank in the Bay of Naples. He forgot Agrippina could swim. Finally, he sent an assassin, and it was lights out for Agrippina. Her ghost apparently haunted him for the rest of his life. Ha! Take that son! Nero spent more time at the chariot races than looking after his Empire. He divorced his first wife, had her beheaded, then married his next wife, whom he later killed. Then, in July of AD 64, Rome caught on fire. Three quarters of the town was burned. Nero blamed the fire on the Christians and either had them thrown in with wild beasts at the Coliseum, or crucified. Others were burned to death, serving as the "lighting" in Nero's gardens. Soon – after a couple rebellions – troops no longer accepted Nero's authority. The Senate condemned Nero to be flogged to death, but he chose to take his own life.

The worst thing that Nero ever did: He performed on stage! In those days, actors and performers were looked down upon, so an emperor performing on stage was an outrage. But Nero loved singing and accompanying himself on the lyre. And since he was the emperor, no one was allowed to leave until he was done. It's what you call a captive audience. Women gave birth during his recitals, and some men pretended to be dead so that they could be carried out. One theater he performed at was knocked down by an earthquake. Apparently even the gods didn't like his singing.

The second-worst thing that Nero ever did: He went to the Olympic Games in Greece. Okay, that doesn't sound terrible, except he actually joined in and won every contest he entered, even a chariot race. (He had fallen out of his chariot, but no one dared pass him.) Scandalous! Oh, and to top it off, while he was gone he left a freedman (someone who used to be a slave) in charge of Rome. As you can imagine, the Romans weren't too happy taking orders from an ex-slave.

Nero really didn't fiddle while Rome burned: you may have heard that rumor, but they didn't have fiddles back then. Lyre's yes, fiddles, no. Instead, he sat on the palace roof singing and playing the lyre and watching the flames. It was kinda like being at a drive-in movie.

Cool fact: There are no cool facts about Nero.

High-school memories: Nero felt lonely at high school. Really lonely, in fact, since he was the only student. He was great at *pila* (ball playing), discus throwing, charioteering, and was also the captain of the cheerleading team. "Let's go, Nero, let's go!" was his favorite cheer.

Interview with Nero: "I don't have time for an interview. I have a party to attend, a crucifixion to organize, a chariot race to win, and I have to gorge myself on grapes, meat, and wine. Oh, and I'm going to do some public singing later. What do you mean I should spend some time running the empire? The empire can run itself!"

Nero's last words: His famous last words were, "*Qualis artifex pereo.*" It's Latin and it means, "What an artist the world loses in me." Yes, poor world. We really miss you, Nero, we do. And we're not just saying that.

The Evil Queen (from Little Snow White)

Age: Yeah, right. You go ask her.

Loves: Looking in the mirror, Snow White's heart (without Snow White attached), dressing up as an old woman, poisoned apples

Hates: Snow White, Snow White, all dwarfs, Snow White

Fashion rating: *A-* Really: queenly gowns, both haughty and a hottie, she *is* the fairest of them all (except for Snow White).

Romantic status: Married

Favorite saying: "Looking glass, Looking glass, on the wall, Who in this land is the fairest of all?"

For those who can't put two and two together: A looking glass is an old fashioned way of saying mirror.

Grimm beginnings: The story of the Evil Queen (and Snow White) comes from the brothers Grimm who lived in the early 1800s. Not only did the brothers have a cool last name, they also had the splendid idea of collecting various fairytales and writing them down so that people like you and I could read them today. The Grimm's version of Snow White was collected from Jeannette and Amalie Hassenpflug – who lived in the town of Cassel. Really that's where they lived and that was their real last name. *Hassenpflug!* It sounds like a swear word. Try it out in gym class. "Oh Hassenpflug! I missed the basket!"

Favorite hangout: Her absolutely fave place to be is inside her glorious palace on the carpet in front of the magic looking glass.

Personality type: The Evil Queen has personality type G – as in she turns green with envy whenever someone more beautiful than she shows up.

Hairstyle: Queen Bee hairstyle

Abilities: To dress up like an old hag, quite a good dancer

Nicknames: Mirror Girl, Heartless One, T.M.E.Q.W.L.I.T.C. (The mean evil queen who lives in the castle)

Name of her autobiography: *Staying Beautiful and raising your EQ* (Evil Queen)

Favorite movies: *Snow White and the Seven Dwarfs*, *Snow White and the Three Stooges*, *Snow White: A Tale of Terror*

A sad tale: Once upon a time a beautiful, wonderful queen married a widowed king. He came with baggage, though – walking, talking baggage named Snow White. She ungratefully grew up to be the most beautiful creature in the land. How unfair! So the queen did the only logical thing she could. She tried to rid the world of Snow White. First, she sent a huntsman to cut out her heart. He didn't have the heart to do it. Then the queen found out that Snow White was housekeeping for seven little dwarfs. (It sounds like a medieval sitcom.) The queen dressed up as an old peddler-woman and laced Snow White's bodice so tightly, she fell to the floor as if dead. The dwarfs came home and cut the laces so Snow White could breathe and continue housekeeping. The queen returned in her disguise and gave Snow White a poisoned comb. Silly Snow white took it and ended up on the floor again. The dwarfs stumbled home and saved Snow White once more. Finally, the queen returned with a poisoned apple. Snow White ate it and dropped down dead. The dwarfs placed her in a glass coffin and a prince came by and asked to have the coffin for his palace (they didn't have plasma TVs back then). His henchmen stumbled over a tree stump, dropped the coffin, and the piece of apple popped out of Snow White's throat. She woke up and next thing you know, she and the prince got married. Meanwhile, the Evil Queen asked her looking glass if she was the fairest of all and it answered, "Oh, Queen, of all here the fairest art thou, But the young Queen is fairer by far as I trow." So, in a rage, the Evil Queen went to visit Snow White. When the Evil Queen arrived she was forced to wear red-hot iron slippers – she danced in them until she died. Don't remember that ending? Old fairytales often weren't as cute as they are made out to be today.

What the Evil Queen did wrong: Everyone knows if you want to get rid of Snow White, you should first bump off the meddling dwarfs. Then there'll be no one to rescue her. And if you have time, send the prince a poisoned apple.

Cool fact: In German, Snow White is called *Sneewittchen*, which means Little Snow White. Sounds like another swear word to me. You Sneewittchen Hassenpflug! Call a classmate that sometime. You'll be laughing all the way to detention.

High-school memories: High School was the greatest time of the Evil Queen's life. Knights slayed dragons just to go on dates with her, and she was voted the best Prom Queen ever (until Snow White came along). On graduation evening she asked the looking glass, "Looking glass, Looking glass, on the wall, Who in my school is the fairest of all?" And the looking glass answered: "Oh Queen, you ain't square, you be the most fair anywhere, woo-ha!" (The looking glass was going through a rap phase back then.)

Why did the queen want to eat Snow White's heart? Easy. In the old days some weird people believed that by eating a person's heart, you would gain the characteristics and powers of that person. Or get a bad case of indigestion.

Interview with the Evil Queen: "Now every-one talks about how beautiful Snow White is. What about her IQ? She was the dumbest crea-ture in all the land. I knew field mice who were smarter. Hey, Snowy, try this poisoned comb. 'Uh, okay, duh, I will.' Hey, how about a poi-soned apple? 'Uh, okay. Duh. Thanks.' She believed the world was flat. And she was a

housekeeper for seven dwarfs. How stupid is that? If only I'd found some stronger poison."

Invention she's been waiting an eternity for: A poisoned apple that actually works.

How to know if you're dating the Evil Queen: She keeps talking to her magic mirror.

Stepmothers, are they really *soooo* bad? Nah. Just this one.

Scarface Capone

Birthdate: January 17, 1899

Deathdate: January 25, 1947

Occupation: Gangster

Favorite city to hangout in: Chicago

Loves: Gambling, the way people call him Mr. Capone, Sir!, corrupt officials, playing banjo, dressing up

Hates: People who call him Scarface, incorruptible officials, attempted assassinations, how snooty Elliot Ness is

Fashion rating: *A* A nice tie! A groovy hat! A Tommy Gun! Snarly, dangerous, yet somehow an all-round friendly guy. How *does* he pull it off?

Personality type: Ruthless, grinning mobster

Birthplace: Brooklyn, New York

Deathplace: His estate in Miami, Florida.

Hairstyle: Balding, combed back gangsta hair. Okay, it did look a little silly, but who would dare to make fun of him?

Romantic status: Married with one kid

Nicknames: Scarface, Snorky, the big fellow

How he got the first nickname: When he was eighteen, Capone insulted the sister of a thug named Frank Gallucio. Frank and Al got in a knife fight which ended with Al getting a deep slash from his right ear to his mouth, leaving a lifelong scar – thus the nickname Scarface. Apparently Al hated the nickname.

How he got the scar, according to him: He got it in World War I as part of the Lost Battalion (a battalion that got lost). Uh, Al, uh, sorry to point this out . . . but you weren't old enough to fight in that war.

How he got the second nickname: Snorky! Who would dare call Al Capone Snorky! Well, apparently Al *liked* that nickname! *Snorky* meant being well-dressed in 1920s' slang. Fashion! That's what it was all about for Al.

How he got the third nickname: The Big Fellow was the name his men used for him.

The story of Scarface: Alphonse Gabriel Capone was born to a barber and a seamstress who lived in Brooklyn. As a teenager, he joined two "kid" gangs – The Brooklyn Rippers and the Forty Thieves Juniors. They specialized in petty crime (not pretty crime, but petty). When he was fourteen, Al threw a female teacher to the ground and was expelled from school (he was in grade six). He never went back. Instead he joined a new gang, Five Points Gang (named after a place in Manhattan where five streets met). A few years later he got married to Mae Coughlin and had a son. Then Al got involved in a fight with a rival gang and he was sent to Chicago to cool off. Instead of cooling off, he became

second in charge, after a gangster named
Johnny Torrio. Torrio was injured in an
assassination attempt, so he went back
to Italy and gave his "business" to Al.
This was when prohibition was in
full force (a time when it was illegal
to sell alcohol, but it was still okay to
dance). That meant there were a lot of
people who wanted alcohol, so Al gladly
sold it under the table. In fact Al got so
good at selling alcohol, gambling, and other dastardly business enterprises that he started making around a hundred
million a year. The courts couldn't stop him because he
would either intimidate witnesses, or bribe officials. He did
have a thorn in his side, though. George "Bugs" Malone was
horning in on Al's territory. So a member of Al's gang, Jack
"Machine Gun" McGurn (what a cute nickname) came up
with a plan to bump off Bugs and several members of his
gang on Valentine's Day. The plot involved luring them to a
warehouse, pretending to be police, then shooting them all
with a Tommy Gun. It worked, too. They ended up "offing"
six rival gangsters and an optician, who just liked to hang out
with gangsters (note to self, don't hang out with gangsters).
They didn't get Bugs, though, because he was late for the
meeting. Still, the Valentine's Day Massacre broke up
Malone's gang (literally), and now Al owned all of Chicago.
The murders made the law want to catch him even more,
but they couldn't pin anything on him. Finally Elliot Ness (A
Prohibition Bureau Agent) and his team of U.S. Treasury

 agents (called the "Untouchables") brought Al Capone in, not for murder, or illegal gambling, or spitting in public, but for the worst, most awful crime imaginable – tax evasion! Al was sentenced to eleven years and was eventually sent to Alcatraz, the toughest prison in the U.S. By the time Al got out, his empire was mostly gone. He retreated to his estate, suffering from dementia, and died there.

Why Al didn't take over the Chicago rackets after getting out of jail: Because he was, as his associate, Jake "Greasy Thumb" Guzik said, "nuttier than a fruitcake."

Favorite saying: "The government can't collect legal taxes from illegal money." Ooops. Turned out he was wrong. They can. They will. They did.

Who put the Tommy in Tommy Gun? The Tommy Gun was actually called the Thompson Submachine Gun after General John T. Thompson (who was driven to invent a hand-held machine gun), and it was used by gangsters and police. It was also sometimes called the Chicago Typewriter and the Chicago Piano.

Favorite movies: *Scarface, The Road to Perdition, Al Capone, The Untouchables, St. Valentine's Day Massacre*

Code of Silence: Gangsters weren't supposed to rat on each other to the cops. In fact, Frank "Tight Lips" Gusenberg, who was shot nineteen times during the Valentine's Day Massacre, lived for a few hours after the attack. When the cops asked him who shot him, he said, "Nobody."

Al "The Banjo" Capone: Al Capone played the banjo for entertainment while in Alcatraz. Remember, they didn't have MP3 players back then.

High-school memories: Al didn't quite make it to high school.

Invention he's been waiting for: He already had it. A Tommy Gun.

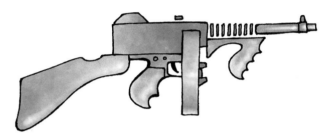

Interview with Scarface: "It's not like I wanted to control the whole world. Just Chicago. Is that so much to ask for? One measly little city. Really, why did everyone get so touchy about a murder here and massacre there? There were still lots of people left in Chicago. And I was just giving the people what they wanted . . . alcohol and gambling."

Scrooge

Age: Old. He put the *senior* in senior citizen and the *gerry* in geriatrics.

Occupation: Businessman

Home: England

Loves: Being miserly, miserable, and mopy.

Hates: Ghostly visitors, when people expect to have Christmas Day off, tipping

Fashion rating: *C-* A ratty greatcoat? Pre-Victorian duds. Hey, if you're rich, you're supposed to flaunt it.

Personality type: Complaining miser with a goodly peppering of grouchiness

Hairstyle: He has slept-on-it-in-my-nightcap hair. And it's old hair. Yuck.

Romantic status: Single. No wonder.

Favorite saying: "Bah! Humbug!" Remember to pause between the two words. Deliver them like ax blows to the greeting of "Merry Christmas."

His favorite quote: "Every idiot who goes about with 'Merry Christmas' on his lips, should be boiled with his own pudding and buried with a stake of holly through his heart." Wow, that's probably the meanest thing ever said in the history of Christmas.

The crotchety story of Scrooge: Charles Dickens (February 7, 1812–June 9, 1870) was an English writer who liked to pen really long novels because he was paid by the word. Finally, he published a short novel (a novella, actually) called *A Christmas Carol* in 1843, which introduced us to Ebenezer Scrooge. Once upon a time, Ebenezer, a kind, intelligent businessman, was nagged by four ghosts. First, the ghost of Christopher Marley, Ebenezer's business associate, dropped by in chains, nagging Scrooge about trying to be a nice guy, or else he'd end up in chains too. The Ghost of Christmas Past nagged him about his past, the Ghost of Christmas Present nagged him about the here and now, and the Ghost of Christmas Future nagged him about – you guessed it – the future. They nagged and nagged and nagged until Scrooge gave away some of his money and a turkey and lived happily ever after.

A Scroogy fact: Ebenezer Scrooge is based on certain Victorian social reformers and businessmen who believed that charity just made people lazy, and that the poor should be left to die because there were already too many people. At least there's no one like that these days, right? Right?

Another Scroogy fact: Scrooge's name inspired by a real life Scottish person – Ebenezer Lennox Scroggie. One day, Charles Dickens stumbled across a headstone in a graveyard that read: *Ebenezer Lennox Scroggie, Mean Man.* So Dickens used the name for his character. Turns out the headstone actually read *Meal* Man, not *Mean* Man. Scroggie was a corn merchant, so he sold corn *meal.* And he was apparently very rambunctious, generous, and a big partyer!

The hum behind Humbug: *Humbug* means "nonsense" or "drivel."

High-school memories: Ebenezer spent nearly all his time at a boarding school. Even Christmas Day, because his dad was too busy to pick him up. Nice dad! Scrooge graduated at the head of his class, getting top marks for miserly conduct.

Interview with Scrooge: "I don't just loathe Christmas – I loathe Easter, birthdays, Hanukkah, St. Patrick's Day, and Halloween. Any day that people celebrate and don't think about the work they should be doing is a useless day! I say banish the word *holiday* from our language. From now on, everyone should work every day from the moment they're born, until they take their last breath."

Invention he's been waiting for: A de-ghost-ifier, and a de-guilter

How to know if you're dating Scrooge: Does he refuse to pay for movies? Dinner? New clothes? Does he say "You remind me of the Ghost of Christmas past"? He's Scrooge.

Other Villains from Dickens's work

That Charles Dickens – what the dickens got into him, eh? Every book he wrote had wonderful villains. Here's a sample:

Fagin: Fagin is the evil character in the novel *Oliver Twist* (1838). Oliver is an orphan who runs away from his terrible job and joins a gang of young criminals. The mastermind is Fagin, an old guy who teaches the kids how to pickpocket and commit other crimes. He lives off their stolen goods. In the end, he gets hanged. Oops.

Bill Sikes: He's also from *Oliver Twist*. He is immensely strong, has a nasty temper and a nasty dog named Bullseye. Sikes put the "syke" in *psycho*. An angry mob chases him and he accidentally hangs himself while trying to get away. *Hmmm*, there seems to be a theme developing here.

Uriah Heep: Hey, with a name like that, this guy has to be bad. Or messy. He's the villain in *David Copperfield* (1850). Mr. Heep is an insincere creep who tries to marry Agnes Wickfield and gain control of the Wickfield fortune. David Copperfield and some other characters stop him and Heep the Creep ends up in prison. Crime doesn't pay!

Miss Havisham: Get this! Miss Havisham fell in love with a dastardly man, who didn't show up for their wedding. Havisham stopped every clock in her mansion and didn't remove her wedding dress for years! That's disgusting, gross, and stinky! She made everyone else's life miserable, including Pip's, the protagonist of *Great Expectations* (1860). When she saw how wrong she was, her wedding dress caught fire and she lapsed into a coma. Nice ending, Dickie.

The Phantom
of the Opera

Age: Really old (40 or 50 years old!)

Occupation: Musician/phantom

Home: Palais Garnier Opera House, nineteenth century Paris

Loves: Christine, setting traps, laughing loudly, popping up out of nowhere, composing long, depressing operas

Hates: Raoul, when people mistake him for an NHL goalie, the way his face sweats behind the mask

Fashion rating: *A+* Mad laughter? Black flowing garments? A stylish mask? The Phantom kicks butt in the fashion parade.

Personality type: Svengali madman musician

Birthplace: A small town not far from Rouen, France

Hairstyle: A phantom comb over

Abilities: Ventriloquism, acrobatics, composing, murder

Romantic status: Single, but looking for a songstress who likes long walks through leaky tunnels, listening to depressing operas, and living underground

Nicknames: Angel of Music, O.G. (Opera Ghost)

Favorite saying: "Look! You want to see! See! Feast your eyes, glut your soul on my cursed ugliness!" He says this every time he takes off his mask. It's a real gas at parties.

Favorite movies: *The Phantom of The Opera*, *The Phantom of the Paradise*, *The Phantom of the Horse Opera* (It has Woody Woodpecker in it. The Phantom busts a gut at that one.)

I bet you say that to all the girls: "Know that I am built up of death from head to foot and that it is a corpse that loves you and adores you and will never, never leave you!" Okay, that's just scary, Mr. Phantom. *S-C-A-R-Y.*

Cool fact: Fans of *Phantom of the Opera* call themselves phans. Ha! That's Phunny! And Phweird!

The phantastically phrightening story of the Phantom: The woeful tale featuring the Phantom can be found in the gothic novel *The Phantom of the Opera* (*Le Fantôme de l'opéra*, 1910) by Gaston Leroux. In it there's the amazing Palais Garnier Opera House, which has been built over an underground lake. The opera house is haunted by the opera ghost who causes a few deaths here and there and blackmails the owners into giving him money and his own private booth in the theater – number five. He falls in love with Christine Daaé, a young singer, and trains her by appearing as a floating voice. She calls him her Angel of Music. He helps her career by causing a few more accidents to happen. Oops, how did that chandelier fall? The dashing Vicomte

Raoul de Chagny (a vicomte is a noble who is above a baron but below an earl) is also in love with Christine. *Hmmm*, I wonder where this'll lead? The Phantom gets angry about Raoul and he takes Christine to his lair beneath the opera house. She sees the real him for the first time – he wears a mask to hide his deformed face, and it turns out his name is Erik. She grabs the mask and gawks at his face, then screams. That's not going to make him feel any better! He lets her go, as long as she promises to come back of her own free will. Instead, she promises herself to Raoul. Before they can get away, the Phantom kidnaps her again. Raoul tries to rescue her but nearly drowns, and it's only after Christine promises to marry the Phantom that he rescues Raoul. Christine willingly kisses the Phantom's forehead and her tears mingle with his. He has a change of heart (he has a heart?) and lets her go with Raoul. The Phantom dies at the end, apparently of a broken heart.

How the Phantom got so phantomly: He was the son of a master masoner, born with a terribly disfigured face. He ran away from home because his parents couldn't look at him, then worked in a sideshow as a living corpse. He picked up ventriloquism, acrobatics, and an obsessive love of music during his traveling life. He became a court assassin for a Persian shah, building traps and some lovely torture devices. The shah decided to bump him off and the Phantom fled to France and became one of the architects of the Palais Garnier Opera House. Which is how he built his lair and all the other secret tunnels that he used to sneak about.

Those wacky authors: Gaston Leroux was a real character! After inheriting over a million francs (francs were French currency) from his father, he started partying, drinking, dancing, and gambling until it was all gone. Clever, Gaston! Luckily, he still had some brain cells left, so he became a journalist and began writing plays and mystery novels. He even started his own film company. Clever, Gaston!

In case you missed it: *The Phantom of the Opera* is an update to the classic fairytale *The Beauty and the Beast*. Oddly enough it is also inspired by George du Maurier's *Trilby*. You know, the book with the hypnotist and the songstress.

You sleep where? The Phantom sleeps in a casket. No, he's not a vampire. He just wants to get used to eternity. Or maybe he's cheap, he's gonna be sleeping in it for the rest of time, he might as well sleep in it while he's alive.

His opera: The phantom wrote his own opera called *Don Juan Triumphant.* He explains it thus: "You see, Christine, there is some music that is so terrible that it consumes all those who approach it." Sounds like country music to me.

What he looks like behind the mask: "Imagine, if you can, Red Death's mask suddenly coming to life in order to express, with the four black holes of its eyes, its nose, and its mouth, the extreme anger, the mighty fury of a demon; AND NOT A RAY OF LIGHT FROM THE SOCKETS." Okay, he got hit with the ugly stick. We get it.

High-school memories: Back then he was known as the Phantom of the High-School Gym. He was always hanging around backstage, using his ventriloquism to scare teachers, popping up in the middle of the gym floor during parades. He made his first mask in shop class and got an *A+*.

Interview with the Phantom: "Ah, music, murder and mayhem. The three *Ms* that make my life happy. Do you know how many chandeliers I've broken in my lifetime? It hasn't been all chuckles. People complain about their jobs, but really, have you ever had to work as *the living corpse*? On minimum wage, too."

How to know if you're dating the Phantom: Does your date keep talking to you out of the shadows? Does he hum a lot and laugh loudly? Does he insist on only going to costume parties? He's the Phantom.

Mephistopheles

Age: He's a devil. He doesn't age.

Occupation: Second-in-command in H-E-Double Hockey Sticks. It's a hot job.

Home: A spiky chair right next to the furnace.

Loves: Nothing

Hates: Everything

Fashion rating: C+ Horns? Smoky, raspy voice? Arched eyebrows? C'mon, you're a walking cliché. Try wearing a nice flamboyant tie. Or a nose ring to accent your flinty eyes. Jeepers! Wake up. The seventeenth century is so over.

Personality type: Devilish swindler

Birthplace: Heaven. Oddly enough, Mephistopheles was an angel before he became a fallen angel.

Romantic status: Eternally single

Sometimes called: Mephisto, Mephistophilus, Mephist, Mephistophilis

Favorite saying: "It's just a soul. It's not like it's worth anything."

Favorite movies: *Faust, I was a Teenage Faust, Needful Things*

Cool fact: Mephistopheles doesn't have any nose hairs because he snorts fire.

The funny, silly, stupid, dumb story of Faust: Mephistopheles first appears in German tales about a "learned" guy named Faust, who wants to trade his soul for power. This story is the inspiration behind Christopher Marlowe's play *The Tragical History of Doctor Faustus* (1604). In the play, Doc Faustus, who is a brainiac, studies every science and math under the sun until he knows the subjects inside out. He becomes frustrated because he can't find the answer to life, so he turns to magic and summons a demon. Uh, bad move. The demon's name is Mephistopheles and he's the right-hand-man to the devil himself (AKA Lucifer, Satan). Faustus offers his soul in trade for twenty-four years on earth with Mephistopheles as his servant to "To giue (give) me whatsoeuer I shal aske, To tel me whatsoeuer I demaund." Didn't they talk funny back then? So Mephistopheles agrees to the deal (after first consulting with his boss). Then you know what Faustus does with all this power? Does he become King of England? Conquer the world? Create a video game company? Nope, he visits the pope, turns invisible, and steals his food. Oh, ha ha! Then he conjures up spirits from ancient Troy. Wow! That was worth selling your soul for. He spends the last year or so of his time on Earth warning people not to sell their souls. Then he takes a trip with Mephistopheles to you-know-where forever. Great plan, Faustus! Guess you weren't so smart in the end.

Bloody fact: Faustus signed his pact with the Devil using his own blood. At first it congealed and he couldn't write his name, but good ol' Mephistopheles brought some hot coals that uncongealed the blood and the pact was signed. Uh, whenever someone asks you to sign a pact in your own blood . . . don't.

What his name means: Mephistopheles is similar to the Greek *Me Fausto Philos* which means "friend of Faustus." Nice friend!

His best friend: Was Beelzebub, one of the devil's lieutenants. Mephistopheles and Beelzebub had a great Abbott and Costello routine called *Who's Burning on First?* They'd repeat it for hours to any newcomers to the land down under.

Other stories about selling your soul to the devil: (You can't swing a dead cat around your head without hitting someone who's tried to sell their soul to the devil.)

The blunder of Theodiphilys: One of the first soul-selling stories is the tale of Theodiphilys, an archdeacon who sold his soul to become bishop. Uh, I think your boss might notice. Theodiphilys repented and got his soul back, then died and became a saint. Not a bad deal.

The master smith: In this Norwegian folktale a master smith makes a deal with the devil to become the greatest smith in the world – "the master over all masters." But God and St. Peter come along and do some amazing smithy tricks (like taking the leg off a horse, fixing its shoe, then putting the leg back on or smithying an old ugly woman into a beautiful young maiden). The smith is given three wishes and he uses them to trick the devil (including trapping him in a purse and hammering on him). The devil becomes so frightened of the smith that he decides not to let him into hell.

The devil went down to Georgia: In this famous song the devil tries to win the soul of a fiddler named Johnny. He sets up a contest where, if Johnny plays the best fiddling music, he wins a gold fiddle. But if the devil plays best, he keeps Johnny's soul. The devil gets a smokin' song off, but Johnny puts his heart into some classic fiddlin' and wins the prize. The devil playing a fiddle? Now that's just silly! What was he thinking? He's much better with a guitar.

The crossroads and the blues: The rumor is that in order to become the greatest blues guitar player ever, all you have to do is go down to the crossroads and promise your soul to the devil. Either that or practice a lot.

High-school memories: Mephistopheles went to high school in heaven and was taught by several saints. He sat at the back and fumed a lot and refused to memorize the Ten Commandments. His report card said, "Most likely to fall from heaven and spend eternity in a hot, hot place."